RAINBOW magic®

The Weather Fairies

Join the **Rainbow Magic Reading Challenge!**

Read the story and collect your fairy points to climb the

Dedicated to Liss Brothwell,
who is a little ray of sunshine

 Special thanks to
Sue Mongredien

ORCHARD BOOKS

First published in Great Britain in 2004 by Orchard Books
This edition published in 2016 by The Watts Publishing Group

29

© 2016 Rainbow Magic Limited.
© 2016 HIT Entertainment Limited.
Illustrations © Georgie Ripper 2004

HiT entertainment

A CIP catalogue record for this book is available from the British Library.

ISBN 978 1 84362 641 1

Printed in Great Britain

MIX
Paper from
responsible sources
FSC® C104740
www.fsc.org

The paper and board used in this book are made from wood from responsible sources

Orchard Books
An imprint of Hachette Children's Group
Part of The Watts Publishing Group Limited
Carmelite House, 50 Victoria Embankment, London EC4Y 0DZ

An Hachette UK Company
www.hachette.co.uk
www.hachettechildrens.co.uk

Goldie
the Sunshine
Fairy

by Daisy Meadows

illustrated by Georgie Ripper

ORCHARD

The Fairyland Palace

Forest

Sweet Factory

The Village Hall

River

Wetherbury Village

Jack Frost's
Ice Castle

een Wood

The Park

Mrs. Fordham's Cottage

Willow Hill

The High St.

The Museum

sty's
use

Fields

Mudhole

N
←W—E→
S

Goblins green and goblins small,
I cast this spell to make you tall.
As high as the palace you shall grow.
My icy magic makes it so.

Then steal Doodle's magic feathers,
Used by the fairies to make all weathers.
Climate chaos I have planned
On Earth, and here, in Fairyland!

Contents

A Sunny Spell

"I feel as if I'm about to melt," said
Rachel Walker happily.

It was a hot summer afternoon and she
and her friend, Kirsty Tate, were enjoying
the sunshine in Kirsty's back garden. A
bumblebee buzzed lazily around Mrs Tate's
sunflowers, and a single breath of wind
whispered through the yellow rose bushes.

The weather had been so warm and
sunny, Mr and Mrs Tate had given the
girls permission to camp
out in the garden that
night. Kirsty looked
up from a jumble
of tent poles and
bright orange
material she was
sorting through. "It's
been a perfect day,"
she agreed. "Let's hope
tonight is perfect, too. I don't fancy
lying out here in the rain, do you?"

Rachel laughed, and started
untangling tent pegs with her friend.
"I think I'd rather have a shower in
the morning, not in the middle of the
night," she agreed.

Kirsty held up some poles. "Right. How do we put this thing together, then?" she asked brightly.

Rachel scratched her head. "Well..." she began.

"Need some help?" came a voice from behind them.

"Dad!" said Kirsty in relief. "Yes, please. We—" She burst out laughing as she looked at her father.

Rachel turned to see what was so funny. She had to bite her lip not to laugh, too. For there, standing in front of them, was Mr Tate, wearing the most enormous sunglasses she had ever seen.

11

Mr Tate was looking very pleased.
He waggled the glasses up and down
on his nose. "Do you like my new
shades?" he asked.

"Well, yes," Kirsty said, trying to
keep a straight face. "They're very...
summery."

Mr Tate knelt down and started
putting the tent together. "The weather
has been strange all week, I didn't know
whether to buy them or not," he said.
"I hope it doesn't start snowing again!"

Rachel and Kirsty looked at each other but didn't say anything. They shared a very special secret. They knew *exactly* why the weather had been so strange – Jack Frost had been messing it all up.

Doodle, the fairy weather-vane cockerel, usually looked after the weather with his seven magic tail feathers. But Jack Frost had cast a spell to make his goblin servants bigger and sent them to steal Doodle's feathers. Without them, the weather had gone completely haywire. Rachel and Kirsty were helping the Weather Fairies to get them back, but until that time, Doodle was just an ordinary iron weather-vane on top of the Tates' barn.

Yesterday, with the help of Pearl the Cloud Fairy, Kirsty and Rachel had returned the Cloud Feather to Doodle. But there were still four feathers left to find.

"There!" said Mr Tate, stepping back and admiring the finished tent. "It's all yours."

"Thanks, Dad," Kirsty said as he walked away. She put two sleeping bags inside the tent and then flopped down on the grass. "Phew!" she whistled. "It's still so hot! I hope it cools down soon, or we'll never be able to sleep in there." Rachel was frowning and looking at her watch.

"Kirsty," she said slowly. "Have you noticed where the sun is?"

Kirsty looked up and pointed. "Right there, in the sky," she replied helpfully.

"Yes, but look how high it is," Rachel insisted. "It hasn't even *started* setting yet."

Kirsty glanced at her watch. "But it's half-past seven," she said. Now she was frowning, too. "So that can't be right."

Rachel had just opened her mouth to
reply, when suddenly there was a loud
Pop! "What was that?" she whispered.

Pop! Pop! Pop!

"It sounds like it's coming from the
other side of the hedge," Kirsty
answered, her eyes wide. "But there's
only a cornfield over there."

Pop! Pop! Pop!

Curiously, the girls peeped over the hedge to see what was making all the noise. And then they both gasped out loud.

Goldie Drops In

"I don't believe it," Kirsty said, rubbing her eyes. "Is that what I think it is?"

Pop! Pop! Pop!

Rachel nodded. "Popcorn," she breathed.

It was an amazing sight. The sun was so hot that the corn in the field was literally cooking – and turning into popcorn!

Both girls stared as golden puffs of corn
bounced everywhere. It was just
as if the field was one
enormous saucepan.
A delicious smell of
popcorn drifted over
the hedge, and both
girls sniffed hungrily.

Kirsty and Rachel looked
at each other, and grinned.

"There's definitely magic
in the air," Kirsty said.

"It must be the goblin
with the Sunshine Feather,"
Rachel agreed, feeling her
heart beat faster with excitement.

Both girls peered hard at the
field, hoping to spot a goblin lurking
somewhere, but it was difficult to see

clearly through the blizzard of popcorn.
It was still tumbling and twirling
in the sky, like a sandstorm.
Rachel suddenly grabbed
Kirsty's hand.
"Look!" she cried.
Kirsty stared.
Darting above the
corn was a twinkling
yellow light. It was
zigzagging through the air
between the flying pieces of
popcorn and heading straight
towards them. As it came
closer, the air above the field
seemed to glitter with a thousand
tiny sparkles. Both girls could see a
pair of delicate golden wings beating
quickly, and the glimmer of a tiny wand.

21

"It's Goldie the Sunshine Fairy," whispered Rachel in delight.

They held their breath as the fairy weaved in and out of the bouncing corn, neatly dodging each piece. Then she swooped down to land on the hedge in front of them. "Phew!" she laughed. "Talk about a bumpy ride!"

Kirsty and Rachel watched as Goldie shook popcorn dust from her glittering, golden-edged wings. Her face was framed by long, curly, blonde hair, and she wore a gauzy dress in fiery reds, yellows and oranges. A tiny gold tiara glinted in her hair and shiny red bangles glimmered on her wrists.

"Hello again," said Goldie. "I've been hearing all about how you've helped Crystal, Abigail and Pearl. You've done brilliantly!"

Rachel and Kirsty grinned at each other proudly.

"The goblin who has the Sunshine Feather can't be far away," Goldie went on, looking up at the sky where the sun was still blazing as brightly as ever.

"That's what we thought," Kirsty said. "There's a farm on the other side of this field. Shall we start looking there?"

"Good idea," Goldie replied cheerfully. But then her face fell as she looked at the cornfield again. Popcorn was still whizzing around like hot white missiles. "Is there another way across the field, though?"

Goblin on the
Loose!

Goldie sighed. "I don't fancy dodging that popcorn again," she said. She leaned back to examine a scorch mark on one of her wings. "I almost burned myself last time."

"There's a lane that runs down the side of the field to the farm," Kirsty told her. "We'll ask Mum if we can go for a quick walk before bedtime."

Minutes later, the three of them were on their way. The air was practically shimmering with heat. There were cracks in the ground where the earth had become hardened by the sun, flowers wilted in the hedgerow, and the grass was turning dry and brown. There

wasn't even the slightest gasp of wind
now. Once they reached the farm, the
girls and Goldie started searching for
the goblin.

First they peeped into the stables.
Two very hot-looking horses were
sheltering from the sun. "Hello," Goldie
said. "I don't suppose you've seen a
goblin hanging around, have you?"

One of the horses shook her mane.

"All we've seen is this stable," she said.
"And there are no goblins in here."

"It's too hot to go out," the other
horse whinnied.

Next the girls and Goldie slipped into the cowshed. The cows were all half-asleep in the heat, and quite grumpy at being disturbed. There was no goblin.

At last the three friends came to the duck pond. They wondered if the goblin might be cooling off in the water, but there was no sign of him – or the Sunshine Feather.

"You should ask the pigs," a duck quacked helpfully from a shady spot in the reeds.

"They've been grumbling all day about something or other. And pigs are nosy. If there's a goblin on the farm, they'll know about it."

Goldie thanked the duck politely.

"I think I can hear the pigs over here," Rachel said, leading the way around the side of the farmhouse.

Soon they could all hear the grunting. The duck was right, the pigs seemed very upset about something. They all turned to look curiously at Goldie, though, when she flew over to speak to them.

Goldie fluttered down to perch on the biggest pig's snout. "What's the problem?" she asked kindly.

The pig squinted at the golden fairy in front of his little blue eyes. "It's like this," he began, in a cross, squeaky kind of voice. "It's been so hot that the farmer topped up the mudhole with water, so that us pigs could keep nice and cool." He twitched his ears indignantly. "But someone else has pinched our spot in the mud – and he won't let us in!"

"It's not fair," a piglet squealed, running up to Rachel and Kirsty. "It's not fa-a-a-air!"

"It certainly isn't," Kirsty agreed, giving him a pat.

"It sounds like just the kind of trick a goblin would play!" Rachel pointed out. "Where is the mudhole?"

The pigs gave directions and the girls set off with Goldie flying above their heads. Rachel crossed her fingers. She felt quite sure that they would find a goblin in the mud. Who else would be mean enough to

stop the pigs from wallowing in their
own mud pool?

They hadn't been walking for very
long when they heard someone singing
in a croaky, tuneless voice:

"I've been having so much fun
Blasting out this golden sun.
It's roasting, toasting, popcorn weather.
Oh, how I love my Sunshine Feather!"

Kirsty, Rachel and Goldie dived behind
a nearby tree at once, and carefully
peeped out. There, right in the middle of
the mudhole, covered in thick, wet mud,
was an extremely cheerful goblin. He
waved the Sunshine Feather in the air as
he sang, and each time it moved, golden
sunbeams flooded from its tip, making
the air feel even hotter.

When he got to the end of his song, he started all over again, splashing his feet in the mud in time to the words. "I've been having so much fun..."

"What shall we do?" Kirsty whispered. The goblin was holding the feather so tightly, it looked like it would be impossible to take it from him.

Goldie twirled around in frustration.

"I hate seeing him with my Sunshine Feather," she muttered, folding her arms across her chest. "Look, he's got it all muddy!"

Rachel frowned. "Maybe we could distract him somehow, then dash over and grab the feather while he's looking the other way."

"I don't fancy dashing through all that slippery mud," Kirsty said quietly, eyeing it doubtfully. "We'll probably fall over. And look, he's right in the middle of it. He'll be able to spot us coming way before we get there."

They drew further away from the mudhole so that they could discuss their next move without fear of the goblin

overhearing. After a few minutes,
Rachel held up a hand. "Ssshh! What's
that noise?" she hissed in alarm.

A Bamboozled Goblin

Kirsty, Rachel and Goldie held their breath as they listened to the strange new sound. It was a loud, wheezing, rumbling kind of noise, somewhere between a grunt and a hiss. Grumble-sshhh, it went. Grumble-sshhh. Grumble-sshhh...

It was coming from the direction of

the mudhole. Kirsty and Rachel crept back to the tree and peeped out from behind it, wondering what sort of terrifying creature they were going to see.

When Rachel saw what was making the noise, though, she had to clap her hand over her mouth to stop herself laughing out loud. The wheezy rumble was nothing more than the goblin – snoring!

"At least he isn't singing any more," Kirsty laughed.

Goldie fluttered her
wings hopefully when
she saw that the
goblin was asleep,
and she flew a little
closer to the Sunshine
Feather. But her face
fell when she saw just
how tightly the goblin
was clutching the feather to

his chest in his sleep. She flew back to
the girls, shaking her head. "If I try and
pull it out of his grasp, he's sure to
wake up," she told them. "How are we
going to get that feather?"

A smile appeared on Kirsty's face.
"Maybe we could..." she began
thoughtfully. Then she grinned broadly.
"Yes! That could work!" she declared.

Without another word, she began running back towards her house. "Back in a minute," she called over her shoulder.

Rachel and Goldie watched her go. They were both dying to know what Kirsty was up to. Luckily, they didn't have to wait long for her return. And when she came back, she looked quite different!

"What *is* she wearing?" Goldie murmured to Rachel as they saw Kirsty running towards them.

"Her dad's sunglasses," Rachel replied, staring at her friend with great interest. She was starting to wonder if Kirsty had been in the sun for too long. Why had she brought the enormous sunglasses with her? And why was she carrying a fishing rod?

Kirsty grinned at the confused expressions on their faces. "I'll explain everything," she promised, reaching up to rest the fishing rod in the tree. "First, we need to shrink to fairy size, Rachel." Both Kirsty and Rachel had been given beautiful gold lockets by the Fairy Queen. Inside each locket was magical fairy dust. A tiny pinch of the sparkling dust was enough to turn the girls into fairies in the twinkling of an eye!

Kirsty and Rachel sprinkled themselves with fairy dust. It glittered a bright sunshine-yellow in the light and then – whoosh – they were getting smaller and smaller

and smaller. The tree next to them became enormous as the girls shrank to the size of Goldie.

Kirsty and Rachel fluttered their wings in delight. They both loved being fairies.

"Now then," Kirsty said. "Fly up to the tree and I'll tell you my plan."

They all perched by the fishing rod, and Goldie and Rachel watched as Kirsty's nimble fingers balanced the sunglasses on the end of the fishing hook.

"We're going to let the fishing line out slowly," Kirsty told them quietly, "and lower the sunglasses onto the goblin's nose."

"Why?" Rachel wanted to know.

"Do you think they'll suit him?" Goldie asked.

Kirsty shook her head, trying not to laugh. "With sunglasses on, everything will look dark to him," she whispered. "With a bit of luck, he'll think the Sunshine Feather has broken!"

Goldie clapped her hands in delight.

"Oh, what a good idea!" she cried. "I do love to play tricks on those mean old goblins."

Very carefully, Kirsty, Rachel and Goldie turned the wheel of the fishing rod and lowered the sunglasses all the way down to the goblin. Kirsty held her breath as the sunglasses landed right on the end of his nose. Perfect!

They reeled in the fishing line and then Goldie waved her wand to release a stream of magical, sunny fairy dust. Little golden sparkles fizzed and popped like firecrackers around the goblin's head until he woke with a start.

He opened his eyes and blinked when he saw that everything seemed to have gone dark. "My feather's broken!" he moaned, giving it a shake. "Shine, you stupid sun!" he commanded.

Of course, the Sunshine Feather wasn't broken at all. As soon as the goblin shook it, the sun shone more brilliantly than ever. But as far as the goblin could see, the world remained in darkness.

He waved the feather again. "I said, shine!" he ordered, in frustration. The sun shone obediently as if it were the middle of the day, but the goblin could see no change. Twice more he shook the feather and twice more the sun shone hotter and brighter, but through the sunglasses, the goblin saw only twilight. As far as he knew, the Sunshine Feather was having no effect. "Broken!" the goblin finally announced crossly, and he threw the feather away in disgust.

Goldie shot out of the tree at once, like a little golden firework. While the goblin was still muttering gloomily to himself, Goldie swooped down and grabbed the feather. "Thank you!" she sang happily, hugging it tightly as she flew back to the girls. Kirsty's plan had worked!

With another sprinkle of fairy dust, Rachel and Kirsty turned themselves human again and started scrambling down from the tree with the fishing rod.

The goblin spotted them and jumped to his feet. As he did so, the sunglasses bounced on his nose. "Sunglasses?" he exclaimed, sounding puzzled as he reached up to grab the glasses. He pushed them onto the top of his head and peered at the girls, blinking in the dazzling sunlight. "You tricked me!" he yelled in fury when he saw Goldie clutching the Sunshine Feather. "Come back with that feather!"

Kirsty and Rachel looked at each
other fearfully. Now that Jack Frost's
goblins were so big, they seemed more
scary than ever. And this one looked
very angry at having been outwitted.

He shook his fist and ran straight
towards the girls.

"*Run!*" shouted Kirsty.

Happy Pigs

Rachel grabbed Kirsty's hand
and they both ran towards the
farmhouse as fast as they could.
The goblin was right behind them,
making a horrible growling sound
in his throat.

"Give me back that feather! Give
it back!" he screamed angrily.

Rachel's heart thumped painfully in her chest as she ran. The goblin was closing on them. She could hear his breathing, hoarse and ragged. The goblin stretched out his hand to grab her and she gasped as she felt his fingertips brush her shoulder.

"Got y—" he began. Then his voice turned from anger to confusion. "Hey! What's happening?"

With a swirl of dancing sunbeams,
Goldie had waved the Sunshine Feather
and pointed it straight at the goblin. At
once, the sun beat down fiercely upon
him – and the thick mud that
smothered him started drying rapidly.
As his legs became stiff and heavy with
the solidifying mud, the goblin slowed.
Then, as the mud set hard, the goblin
found he couldn't move at all.

"No-o-o-!" he wailed in despair.

Despite having been so scared just a few seconds earlier, the girls found themselves smiling at the sight of the goblin. "He's a goblin statue!" Rachel exclaimed, laughing.

Only his eyes moved now. They flicked back and forth wildly as the goblin glared first at the girls, and then at Goldie who was fluttering beside them. Kirsty noticed her dad's sunglasses on top of the goblin's head. She took a cautious step towards him. And another. The goblin remained motionless, so she marched right up to him and carefully took the glasses.

"I'll have these back now, I think,"
she said. "If I'd known how useful
these sunglasses would be, I'd never
have laughed at Dad for wearing
them!" she told Rachel.

Goldie and the girls made their way
back to the farmhouse where the pigs
were waiting expectantly.

"The mudhole is all yours again,"
Goldie said to the pigs in her sweet
silvery voice. "You'll find a new goblin
scarecrow nearby," she added. "But
don't worry. He won't be in any hurry
to go back into the mud."

The pigs grunted joyfully and started trotting off in search of their cool mud pool. The smallest piglet nuzzled around Kirsty and Rachel's legs before he went. "Thank you," he squealed happily.

Rachel watched them go. "What will happen to the goblin?" she asked. "He won't have to stay there for ever, will he?"

Goldie's eyes twinkled mischievously. "Not for ever, no," she said. "He'll get out of the mud as soon as it rains." She smiled cheerfully. "Jack Frost won't be pleased with him when he finds out we've got the Sunshine Feather back, though!"

Twilight Magic

Now that they were out of danger, Goldie waved the Sunshine Feather with an expert flourish and the sun began to set – just as it was supposed to. The girls watched as the sky was flooded with orange and pink and a rich deep red.

"Let's take the Sunshine Feather back

65

to Doodle," Kirsty said happily. "And then we'd better go to bed!"

Rachel was yawning. "It's been another busy day, hasn't it?" she smiled.

With the sun setting, the warmth was quickly ebbing away and the girls soon found themselves shivering in their thin T-shirts. Goldie fluttered above them with the Sunshine Feather, tapping it gently to sprinkle a few sunbeams onto their bare arms to keep them warm.

It was almost dark by the time they got back to Kirsty's garden. They could just about see the silhouette of Doodle perched on the barn roof.

Goldie flew up to give the cockerel back his magic feather. As she did so, Doodle came to life, his fiery feathers glowing brilliant colours in the twilight. He turned to look at Rachel and Kirsty. "Will come—" he squawked urgently. But, before he could say any more, the magic drained away, his colours faded and he became a rusty old weather-vane once again.

Each time the girls managed to
return one of Doodle's feathers, the
cockerel came to life for a few brief
moments and squawked a couple
of words. Rachel frowned as she
pieced together all the words that
Doodle had said to them so far.
"Beware! Jack Frost will come..."
she murmured, feeling an icy shiver
down her spine as if Jack Frost
was already there. "It's a warning,
Kirsty. Let's hope he's not coming
soon!"

Goldie looked worried. "Take care,
girls. And thank you for everything,"
she said. She blew them a stream
of fairy kisses that sparkled in the
darkening sky. "I must go back
to Fairyland now. Goodbye!"

Kirsty and Rachel watched Goldie fly
away until she was nothing more than
a tiny golden speck in the distance.
Then, just as they were about to get
ready for bed, they heard footsteps and
Mr Tate came out of the house. He
was looking around, a puzzled
expression on his face. "Did I just hear
a cockerel crowing?" he asked.

"A cockerel? At this time of day?" Kirsty replied innocently.

Mr Tate frowned. "I must be hearing things," he said, turning to go back inside. "Good night, girls. Sleep well." Then he glanced up at Doodle as he headed back towards the house. "I'm sure that weather-vane had a smaller tail," he muttered, then shook his head. "Seeing things as well! Definitely time to call it a night..."

Kirsty and Rachel smiled at each other. "Only three more feathers to find," Kirsty said. "I wonder which one will be next!"

Now it's time for Kirsty and Rachel to help...

Evie the Mist Fairy

Read on for a sneak peek...

"Wake up, sleepy head!" cried Kirsty Tate to her friend, Rachel, as she jumped out of bed and started to dress.

Rachel Walker was asleep in the spare bed in Kirsty's room. She was staying with Kirsty and her parents in the village of Wetherbury. Sleepily, she rolled over and opened her eyes. "I was dreaming that we were back in Fairyland," she told Kirsty. "The weather was topsy-turvy – sunny and snowing all at the same time – and Doodle was trying to sort it out." Doodle, the fairies' magic weather cockerel, had been on Rachel's mind a lot lately, because she and Kirsty were on an important fairy mission!

Each day in Fairyland, with the help of the Weather Fairies, Doodle used his magic tail feathers to organise the weather. Each of the seven magic feathers controlled a different kind of weather, and each of the seven Weather Fairies was responsible for working with one feather in particular. The system worked perfectly until mean old Jack Frost sent seven goblins to steal Doodle's magic feathers.

The goblins ran off into the human world with one feather each, and when poor Doodle followed them out of Fairyland, he found himself transformed into a rusty metal weather-vane. The Queen of the Fairies had asked Rachel and Kirsty to help find the magic feathers and return them to Doodle.

Meanwhile, Fairyland's weather was all mixed up – and the goblins had been using the feathers to cause weather chaos in the human world too.

"Poor Doodle," Kirsty said, looking out of the window at the old barn where the cockerel was perched. Her dad had found Doodle lying in the park, and thinking he was an ordinary weather vane, Mr Tate had brought him home and put him on the barn roof.

"Hopefully we'll find another magic feather today," Kirsty continued. "We've already found four of the stolen feathers. We just need to find the other three and then Doodle will get his magic back."

"Yes," Rachel agreed, brightening at the

thought. "But I have to go home in three days, so we don't have long!" As she gazed out at the blue sky, a wisp of silvery mist caught her eye. "Look, that cloud is shaped just like a feather!" she said.

Kirsty looked where Rachel was pointing. "I can't see anything."

Rachel looked again. The wispy shape had vanished. "Perhaps I imagined it," she sighed, turning away to dress.

The memory of the dream fizzed in her tummy like lemonade bubbles. It felt like a magical start to the day.

She loved staying with Kirsty and sharing fairy adventures with her. The girls had met whilst on holiday on Rainspell Island with their parents.

That was when they had first helped the fairies. On that occasion, Jack Frost had cast a nasty spell to banish the Rainbow Fairies from Fairyland, and the girls had helped all seven of them get safely home...

Read Evie the Mist Fairy to find out what adventures are in store for Kirsty and Rachel!

Meet the
Friendship Fairies

When Jack Frost steals the Friendship Fairies' magical objects, BFFs everywhere are in trouble! Can Rachel and Kirsty help save the magic of friendship?

www.rainbowmagicbooks.co.uk

Calling all parents, carers and teachers!
The Rainbow Magic fairies are here to help
your child enter the magical world of reading.
Whatever reading stage they are at, there's
a Rainbow Magic book for everyone!
Here is Lydia the Reading Fairy's guide to
supporting your child's journey at all levels.

Starting Out

Our Rainbow Magic Beginner Readers are perfect for first-time readers who are just beginning to develop reading skills and confidence. Approved by teachers, they contain a full range of educational levelling, as well as lively full-colour illustrations.

Developing Readers

Rainbow Magic Early Readers contain longer stories and wider vocabulary for building stamina and growing confidence. These are adaptations of our most popular Rainbow Magic stories, specially developed for younger readers in conjunction with an Early Years reading consultant, with full-colour illustrations.

Going Solo

The Rainbow Magic chapter books – a mixture of series and one-off specials – contain accessible writing to encourage your child to venture into reading independently. These highly collectible and much-loved magical stories inspire a love of reading to last a lifetime.

www.rainbowmagicbooks.co.uk

"Rainbow Magic got my daughter reading chapter books. Great sparkly covers, cute fairies and traditional stories full of magic that she found impossible to put down" - Mother of Edie (6 years)

"Florence LOVES the Rainbow Magic books. She really enjoys reading now" - Mother of Florence (6 years)

The Rainbow Magic
Reading Challenge

Well done, fairy friend – you have completed the book!
This book was worth 5 points.

See how far you have climbed on the
Reading Rainbow opposite.

The more books you read, the more points you will get,
and the closer you will be to becoming a Fairy Princess!

How to get your Reading Rainbow
1. Cut out the coin below
2. Go to the Rainbow Magic website
3. Download and print out your poster
4. Add your coin and climb up the Reading Rainbow!

There's all this and lots more at
www.rainbowmagicbooks.co.uk

You'll find activities, competitions, stories, a special
newsletter and complete profiles of all the
Rainbow Magic fairies. Find a fairy with your name!